A Penny In My Pocket

C.M. Harris

Nareh Grigoryan

A Penny In My Pocket
by C.M. Harris

Published by Purple Diamond Press 2021
Villa Park, CA

Illustrated by Nareh Grigoryan
Edited by Rebecca Frazer & Brooke Vitale

Paperback: ISBN: 978-1-7355372-6-9
Hardcover: ISBN: 978-1-7355372-3-8

Library of Congress Control Number: 2021909903

Purple Diamond Press, LLC
PO Box 5357, Orange, CA 92863

Visit www.CMHarrisBooks.com for more information
This book can be purchased directly from the author.
Special discount for large quantities for schools/organizations.
info@PurpleDiamondPress.com

A Penny In My Pocket

Mommy and Stevie were on their weekly shopping trip.

Stevie watched Mommy add yummy treats
to the shopping cart:

popcorn and animal crackers for
snack time,

fun pool toys for Stevie's birthday
next week,

and squeaky bones for Sammy—the
family's curly-tailed, white poodle.

5

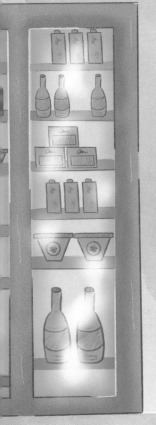

Stevie squirmed around in his seat, stretching his arms toward the shelves.

"Can I have that box of cereal?"

"No sweetie."

"Can I have that RED bag of chips?"

"Can I have that YELLOW balloon?"

"Can I have that fuzzy GREEN blanket?"

"No sweetie."

"Can I have that BROWN chocolate bar?"

"Can I have that PURPLE dino?"

"Can I have that PINK pack of gum?"

"No sweetie."

9

Stevie crossed his arms. "It's not fair," he pouted. "Why can't I have it? You get to buy what you want. Why can't I get what I want? Don't you have money?"

"Yes, my dear Stevie," Mommy said. "I do have money, but we are here to buy the things we need. You may want another dino, but you don't need one. You already have four at home. If we bought everything we wanted, we wouldn't have enough for what we need."

Stevie was very confused. "Mommy, what do you mean?"

"Well, Stevie, your Daddy and I go to work and earn money."

"Like when I do my chores and I get a dollar?" Stevie asked.

"Yes, exactly!" agreed Mommy. "You earn money just like us."

"And I put it in my piggy bank to save it!" Stevie said.

"That's right," Mommy said. It's important to save the money that you earn. That way you're prepared," Mommy continued.

Stevie watched as mommy added bright green, yellow, orange, and red fruits and vegetables to their cart.

"Prepared for what?" he asked.

13

"What if I used all our money to buy toys?" Mommy asked.
"How would we have enough to buy food? Daddy and I prepare by knowing what we need to buy before we spend on what we want."

Stevie thought back to the scrumptious breakfast he had that morning. Not having pancakes for breakfast would make him so sad!

14

Then he remembered a man he'd seen sitting outside the store. He wondered what he'd had for breakfast.

"Mommy," Stevie said. "What if my piggy gets full? What else could I do with my money? Can we eat the money?" He asked.

Mommy looked at Stevie in confusion.

Stevie laughed and his cheeks turned as red as cherry tomatoes.

"Just kidding!" he said. "I did lick a penny before though—it tasted icky!"

"Oh, goodness, my silly Stevie," Mommy giggled. "Please do not put money in your mouth anymore, but that is a good question."

"If your piggy gets full then you can get another bank and continue saving..., or you can buy the purple dino if you saved enough money ..., or you can also donate money to people who do not have much or any money at all..."

"That's a funny word. What is donut-ing?" Stevie asked.

"That does sound like a big word, huh?" Mommy said, while making a silly face.

19

"Donating is when you give away items you do not use anymore, like clothes, toys, or shoes. You can also donate money to a..."

"I know, oooh, I know, Mommy! People donate money to a charity!" Stevie shouted. Then, as quietly as he could, he added, "Charities help people who are poor, right?"

Mommy chuckled. Stevie was excited he knew the answer.

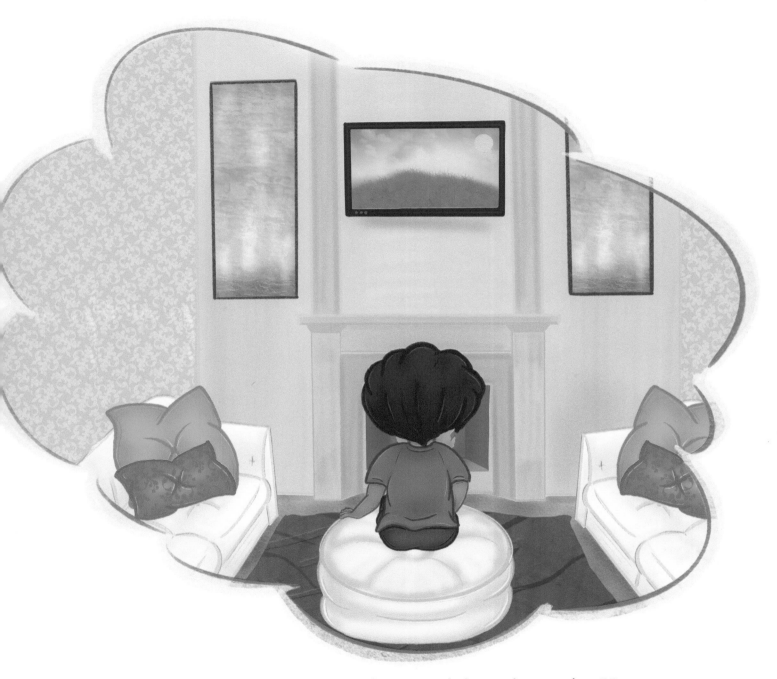

"Yes, my darling," she replied. "How did you know that?"

"I saw it on my cartoons!"

As Mommy checked out,
Stevie thought about what she'd said.
He realized now how lucky he was.

They had enough money to buy
the things they needed—and even
some things they wanted.

22

"Mommy, can I have five dollars?" Stevie asked.

"No Stevie, I just told you that money is earned and..."

"But Mommy," Stevie interrupted. "I want to donate money to the man sitting outside. I don't think he can buy the things he needs."

Stevie's head drooped as he checked his pockets.
"I ONLY HAVE A PENNY IN MY POCKET."

Mommy looked at sweet Stevie and smiled.
"Yes, my sweetheart, I can give you five dollars."

As they left the store, Mommy reached into her purse and proudly handed Stevie the money.

Stevie grabbed her hand, too nervous to move. Mommy smiled as she nudged him forward.

"Here you go, sir," Stevie said, and handed the man a green five dollar bill and his shiny gold penny. "I hope you have a good day."

The man gave Stevie a SMILE.

Stevie happily jumped back into the shopping cart and they headed to the car.

28

Mommy's heart was full of joy. Smiling, she hugged Stevie, "How about we go get some well earned ice cream?"

The Author

C.M. Harris is a children's picture book author writing stories that motivate and inspire young minds. Charity focuses on writing stories that embrace our differences and leaves readers with a lesson to ponder. Award-winning author of **What If We Were All The Same!** she spent her childhood worrying what other kids thought about her due to being diagnosed with Charcot Marie-Tooth Disease at the age of seven. She wrote A Penny In My Pocket to introduce children to the act of giving, saving, and more.

Charity lives in Southern California and enjoys visiting schools where she spreads the importance of friendship, acceptance, and inclusion. Charity loves working with children and was a private tutor for over ten years.

To read more about Charity's journey, visit **www.CMHarrisBooks.com**.
The author can be contacted by email at books@cmharrisbooks.com

May you be so kind and write an Amazon review, every review is appreciated and helps very much.

Check out my other books ↘

Money Tip$

In the story, Stevie wanted to put fun and yummy treats in the shopping cart but Mommy said no and taught him the difference between need and want. Did you know that you can also spend money, save money, and you can even use it to help others too?

Tips To Earn Money
- ask your parents if you can earn money for getting good grades
- ask your parents if you can earn an allowance for doing chores
- start a small business. (sell lemonade, sell handmade crafts, have a yard sale)

Tips To Save Money
- Spend smart, buy items you need before buying the items you want
- Get a savings jar and save half the money you earn (or a piggy bank)

Helping Others
- Donate unused items like toys before buying more toys
- Start a "Giving Jar" (save and find a charity or person in need to donate to)

I'm Saving My Money To Buy _____

I Can Help Someone By _____

Lightning Source UK Ltd.
Milton Keynes UK
UKHW050935090223
416724UK00002B/49